Art and Craft ADVENTURES 2

Mary Carroll • Katie Long

THE O'BRIEN PRESS
PINE FOREST ART

First published 2001 by The O'Brien Press Ltd.
20 Victoria Road, Dublin 6, Ireland
Tel. +353 1 4923333; Fax. +353 1 4922777
e-mail: books@obrien.ie
website: www.obrien.ie
Co-published with Pine Forest Art Centre

ISBN 0-86278-684-3

British Library Cataloguing-in-publication Data
A catalogue reference for this title is available from the British Library

1 2 3 4 5 6 7 8 9 10
01 02 03 04 05 06 07 08

Cover and prelims layout and design: The O'Brien Press Ltd.
Photographs: Dennis Mortell
Colour separations for cover: C&A Print, Ireland
Printed in Italy

CONTENTS

Spiders

Trouble Shooter

Make sure the glue has dried before bending the legs into shape.

Materials

- Cotton balls
- Pipe cleaners
- Coloured paper
- Elastic thread
- Glue
- Felt-tip pens

Equipment

- Scissors

1 Bend four pipe cleaners in half.

2 Glue them into the hole in the centre of the cotton ball.

3 Draw the face on the cotton ball.

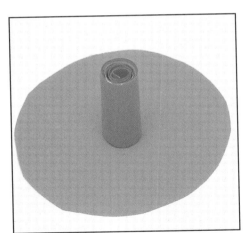

4 Bend out the legs and feet and attach elastic thread to the top of the head with a strong glue.

5 Cut out a circle of paper. Roll up a strip and glue it on top to make a hat.

6 Glue the hat in place and add any other decorations you choose.

Trees

Materials

- Paper
- Paint
  or
- Printing ink
- Corrugated card
- Corks
- Wooden skewer
  or
- Pencil

Equipment

- Newspaper
- Scissors
- Paintbrush
- Container of water
  and
- Tissue or rag (to clean the end of the cork if you want to use it for another colour)

Method

Try out the various shapes by pressing the cork, card and the end of the skewer into the paint and then onto a piece of scrap paper. When you are satisfied that you can get a nice clear print, make pictures by combining the printed shapes on a piece of paper.

Preparation

Cover the working surface with newspaper. Leave yourself plenty of space. Cut the card into strips of varying widths between 1cm and 8cm wide with the corrugations at the ends of the strips.

Cut the strips into lengths, approximately 6cm. Squeeze the paint onto several paper plates or tiles, one plate for each colour. Spread the paint out evenly with the paintbrush to make a flat bed to press the cork or card into.

Trouble Shooter

You can make a lot of prints in quite a short time so you need to have laid out lots of newspaper to put them on to dry. Have extra pieces of card as it can get soggy if it is used a lot.

Printed Blossom Tree

1 Make the trunk of the tree by printing a strip of card about 9cm wide several times, narrowing in towards the top so that it looks like a very steep mountain.

5 Do the same with the medium green and then with the light green. Put lots of light green prints at the top of the tree where the sun would be shining on the leaves.

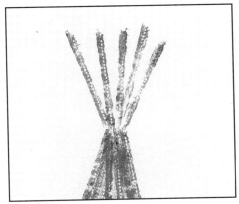

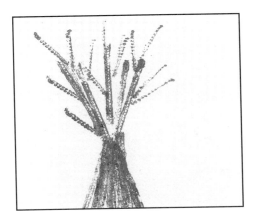

2 From the top of the trunk print about five more spread out like the fingers of a hand, to make branches.

3 Take some narrower pieces of card and print them coming out of the big branches to make smaller ones.

4 Make three different colours of green on your 'green' plate, a light one (add white or yellow or both), the standard one from your paints and a dark one (add a little bit of black or brown). Press the cork into the dark one and dab it all over the branches.

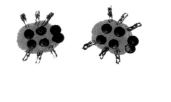

6 Press the end of the skewer into the white paint and print little clusters of blossoms. Make some pink by adding a tiny little bit of red to some of the white and print some more blossoms.

7 With the narrower pieces of card, print some grass around the bottom of the tree, using different greens.

8 With the end of the skewer print some flowers in the grass.

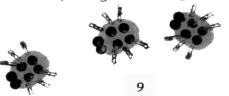

Chicken

Materials
- Card
- Paper
- Felt-tip pens
- Glue

Equipment
- Scissors
- Stapler

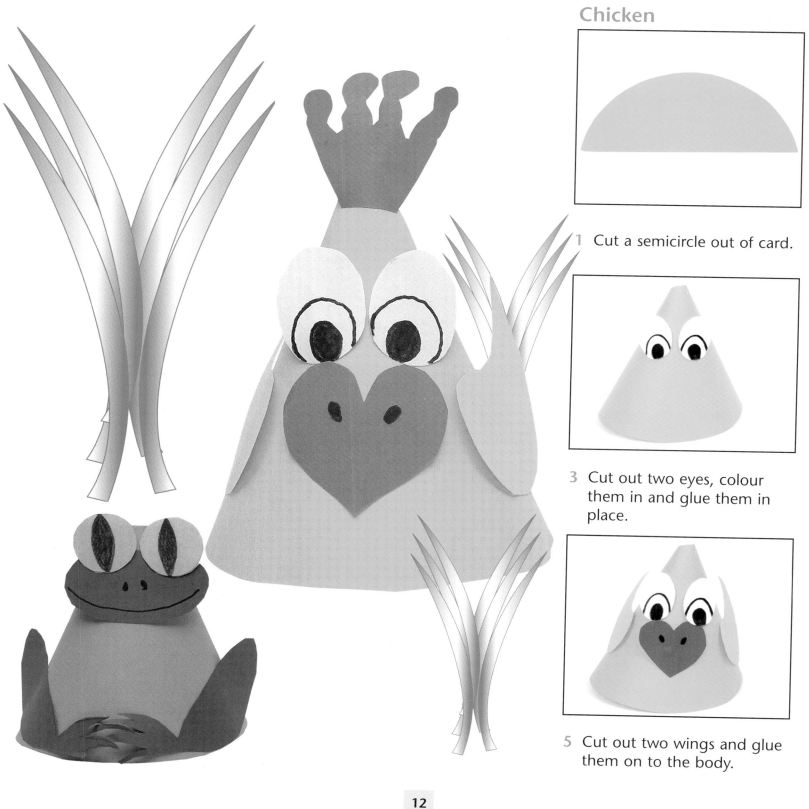

Chicken

1 Cut a semicircle out of card.

3 Cut out two eyes, colour them in and glue them in place.

5 Cut out two wings and glue them on to the body.

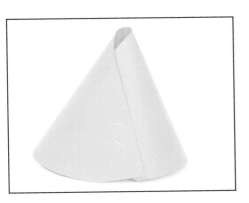

2 Fold it into a cone and staple it.

4 Cut out a large beak and glue it in place.

6 Cut out the chicken's crown and glue it on top of his head.

Butterfly Picture

Materials

- Brightly coloured felt
- PVA glue, copydex or similar fabric glue
- Paper
- Pencil
  or
- Chalk

Equipment

- Scissors

Preparation

Make sure your work surface is very clean. Have plenty of room so that when you lay out your pieces of felt you can choose the contrasting colours easily. Keep the glue well away from the felt until you are ready to use it.

Method

Follow the step-by-step method for the butterfly, adapting it to your own choice of picture.

Butterfly

1 Choose your background colour and lay it flat.

2 Choose a piece of contrasting colour, smaller than the background. If you are making a butterfly picture you will want the wings to match, so fold it in half. Draw half a butterfly shape with the body on the fold.

3 Cut it out double and open it out. Lay it on the background. Cut circles, bars and other shapes out of contrasting colours. Cut them out double as well.

4 Arrange the cut shapes on each wing so that they match.

5 Add another layer of shapes on top of the first layer, once again contrasting the colours. Stick each piece in place, starting from the bottom.

 # Brooches

Materials
- Polymer clay
- Brooch backs
- Glue

Equipment
- Wooden skewer
- Baking tray
- Oven
- Knife

Bear Head

Preparation
Pre heat the oven to 130°C/ 265°F/Gas mark 1.

1   Roll a piece of red clay into a ball.

Trouble Shooter

Make sure the brooches do not touch each other on the baking tray or they will stick together. When cooked, do not touch them until they have cooled down as it is in the cooling period that they go hard. Do not increase the oven temperature as the polymer clay will burn up.

2 Flatten it into a disc for the background.

3 Make a smaller yellow disc and place it on top of the red one.

4 Make a brown disc for the head and place it on top of the yellow.

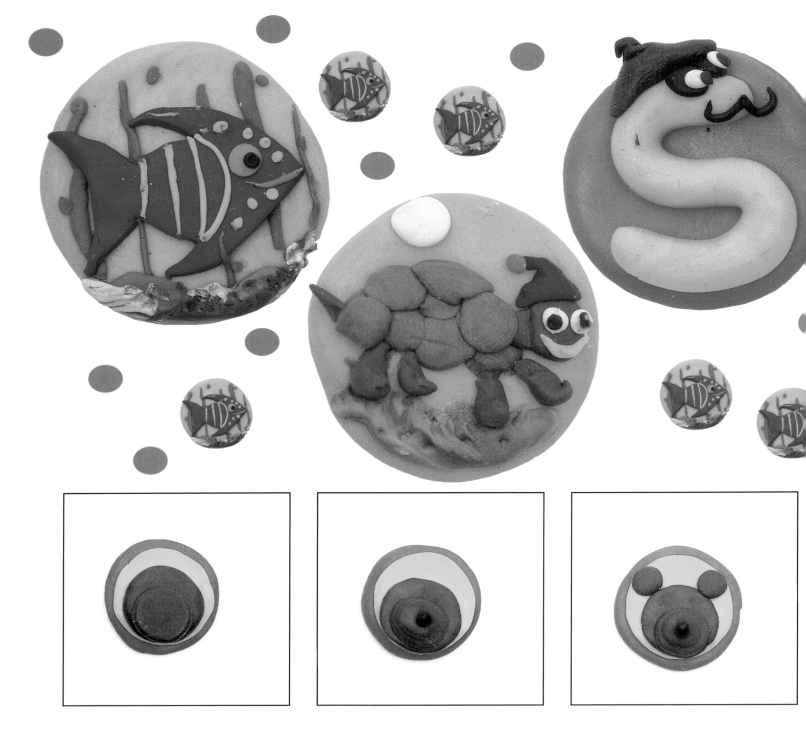

5 Make a smaller brown disc for the cheeks.

6 Make a little brown disc for the snout and a black ball for the nose.

7 Make two ears and attach them.

8 Make two eyes and attach them.

9 Add on any extra decorations of your choice – tongues, ties, hats, etc.

10 Place on a baking tray and bake for 15 minutes. Let it cool down, then glue on a brooch back.

Faces

Materials
- Coloured paper
  or
- Light card
- Pencil
- Glue

Equipment
- Scissors

Trouble Shooter

Cut out all the sections first and then glue everything in place to make the face.

21

Jester

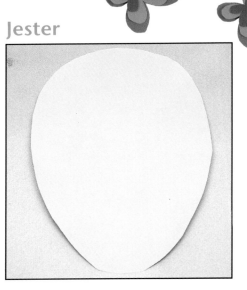

1 Cut out a large oval for the face.

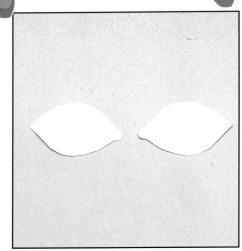

2 Cut out two white eye shapes.

3 Cut out two blue circles and glue them on top of the white ones.

7 Cut out the shape of a moustache, eyebrows and a beard.

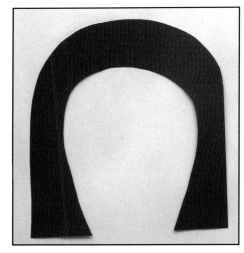

8 Cut out the shape of the hair.

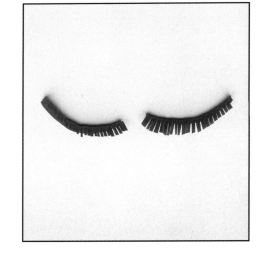

9 Cut two strips of black for eyelashes. Snip small cuts all the way along them and curl them up around a pencil.

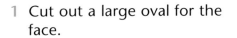

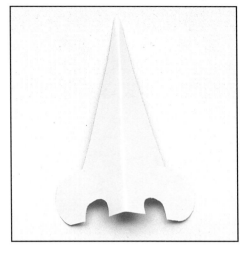

4 Cut out two black circles and glue them on top of the blue ones.

5 Cut out a nose shape, fold it down the centre to make it stand out.

6 Cut out lips and make a cut across the centre to open them.

10 Cut out three of the above shape and glue circles on the ends to make the hat.

11 Cut out a red frill and a green frill. Glue one on top of the other. Glue little circles on the ends to make the neck frill.

12 Assemble the face and glue everything in place.

Dough Boy

Materials

- 4 cups of flour
- 2 cups of salt
- Water to mix
- Acrylic paint, if painting

Equipment

- Large bowl
- Wooden spoon
- Rolling pin
- Board for rolling out the dough
- Jug for water
- Cup for measuring
- Cooking foil
- Baking tray

Preparation

Wear an apron.
Lay out all your materials.

Suggested Themes

House
Owl
Duck
Basket of flowers
Wreath of fruit
Boat
Baby in a cradle

Method

Measure out the flour and salt into the bowl. Mix them together with the wooden spoon. Stir in $\frac{1}{4}$ cup of water. Knead the dough into a ball with your hands; if it is too sticky add some more flour. If the dough doesn't stick together properly, very carefully add a little more water.

Dough Boy

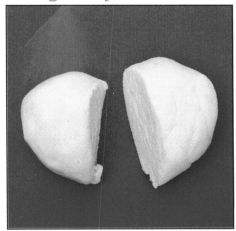

1 Take a lump of dough about the size of a grapefruit. Divide it in two and put one piece aside for steps 5 to 8.

2 Take the other piece and roll with a rolling pin or flatten with your hand to about 1cm thick. Make a rectangle for the body, and two small and two larger rectangles for the sleeves and the trouser legs.

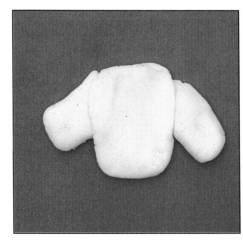

3 Add the sleeves on to the body, pressing them well in so that they are firmly attached.

4 Place the trouser legs in position, lay the body part on top and press it on firmly as with the sleeves.

5 Take a small piece of the dough you have put aside for steps 5 to 8 and roll a ball for the head. Flatten it to 1cm.

6 From the remaining dough make eyes, ears, mouth and nose and press firmly in place.

25

Trouble Shooter

Use plain flour or the model will rise in the oven. Bake your models within 48 hours of making them or they may go mouldy. Even after they are baked don't store your models in a damp place. Leave some space between your models on the baking tray as they will swell and bulge a bit.

7 Add a hat to the head and hair if you wish.

8 Cover a baking sheet with cooking foil. Lay your Dough Boy and any other models you have made on it.

9 Bake in a very cool oven, about 150°C/300°F/gas mark 2, for 12 hours or longer until thoroughly dried out.

10 You can paint your Dough Boy with acrylic paints if you wish or leave him a golden-brown baked colour.

Fish

Materials

- Coloured paper strips 1.5cm x 21cm long
- Glue
- Thread
- Pencil

Equipment

- Scissors
- Pin

Spiral

Roll a strip up around a pencil. Take it off and let it spin out to form a spiral. Then glue the end.

Teardrop

Follow the instructions for the spiral and then pinch one end to form a teardrop.

Zigzag

Fold the strip into a zigzag, using large and small folds.

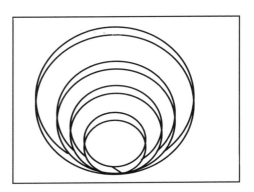

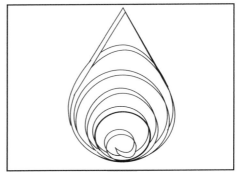

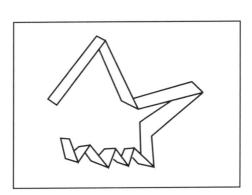

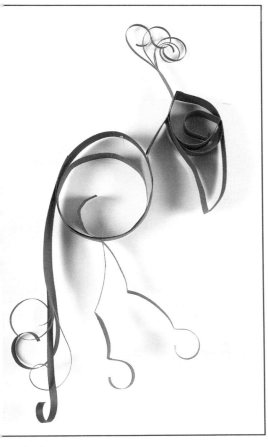

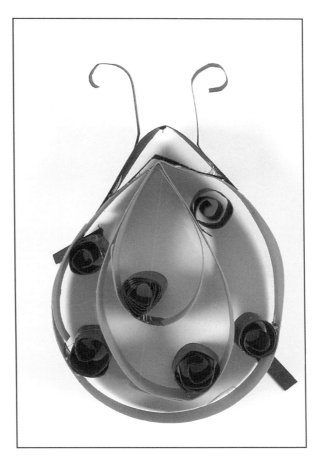

Trouble Shooter

Have all the sections made up before you glue them together.

Fish

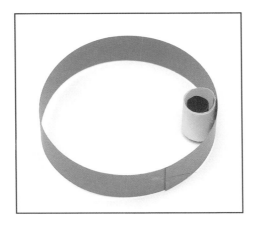

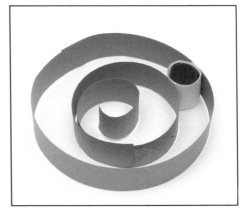

1 Make a circle.

2 Roll up a small spiral and glue it in place for the eye. Add a second small one if you choose.

3 Roll up a spiral and glue it in the centre to make the tummy.

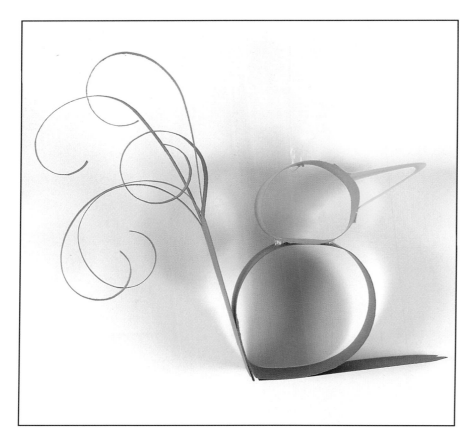

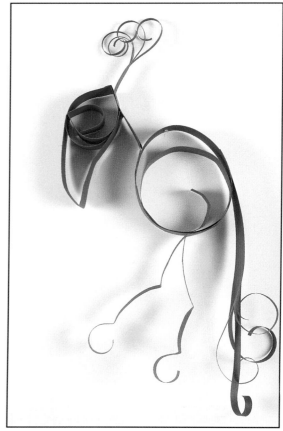

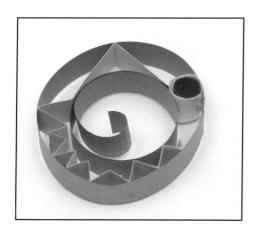

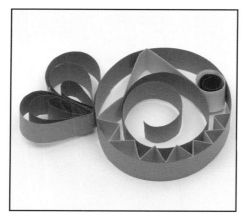

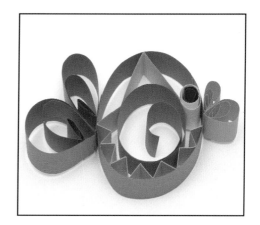

4　Fold up a zigzag and glue it in place.

5　Make two large teardrops. Glue them together and attach them to make the tail.

6　Make two small teardrops for the mouth and glue them in place.

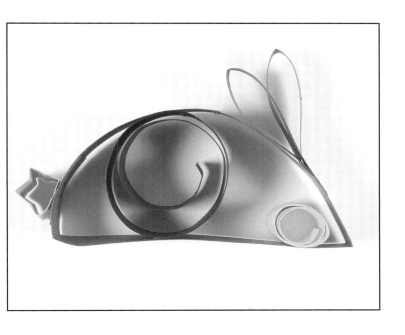

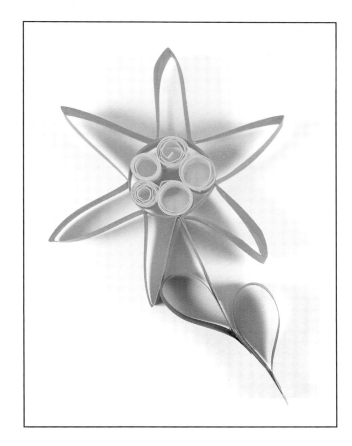

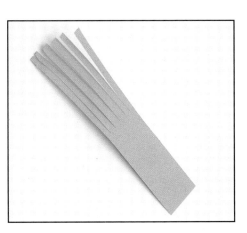

7 Take a strip and make cuts in it to make a fin.

8 Curl the cuts up around a pencil. Glue the fin in place.

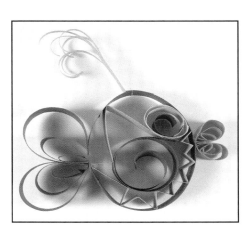

9 Make a hole in the top with a pin and hang up your fish by threading a length of thread through it.

Notes for Teachers

Pages 4–5 SPIDERS
- **Concept** – awareness of form
- **Strand skill** – making constructions
- **Aim** – 'awareness of the three-dimensional nature of form in the visual environment'

Pages 6–9 TREES
- **Concept** – awareness of shape, pattern and rhythm
- **Strand skill** – making prints
- **Aim** – 'experimenting with pattern, understanding the image-making processes'

Pages 10–13 CHICKEN
- **Concept** – awareness of form
- **Strand skill** – making constructions
- **Aim** – 'beginning to develop a practical understanding of structure through construction activities'

Pages 14–15 BUTTERFLY PICTURE
- **Concept** – awareness of pattern and rhythm, colour and tone
- **Strand skill** – creating in fabric
- **Aim** – 'exploring and discovering the possibilities of fabric and fibre as a medium for imaginative expression'

Pages 16–19 BROOCHES
- **Concept** – awareness of shape and form, colour and tone
- **Strand skill** – developing form in (polymer) clay
- **Aim** – 'using an additional way of exploring form'

Pages 20–23 FACES
- **Concept** – awareness of shape, colour and tone
- **Strand skill** – colouring, using coloured paper as a medium
- **Aim** – 'exploring the relationship between the parts and the whole form'

Pages 24–27 DOUGH BOY
- **Concept** – awareness of form
- **Strand skill** – developing form in dough
- **Aim** – 'exploring and discovering the possibilities of (dough as) a medium for imaginative expression'

Pages 28–31 FISH
- **Concept** – awareness of pattern and rhythm
- **Strand skill** – making constructions
- **Aim** – 'exploring and experimenting with the properties and characters (of card strips) in making structures'